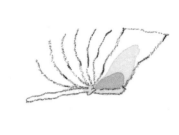

Daddy's zigzagging Bedtime Story

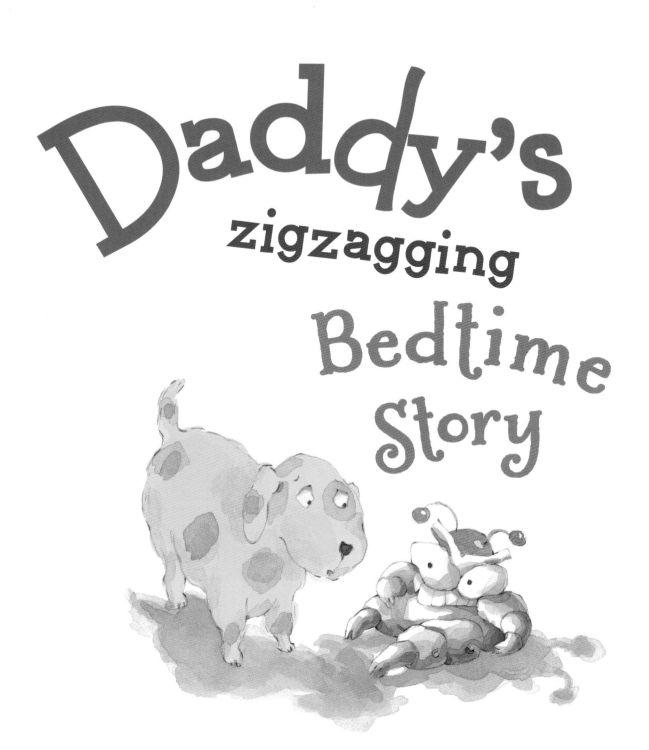

by Alan Lawrence Sitomer

Illustrated by Abby Carter

Disney · HYPERION BOOKS

NEW YORK

Printed in Malaysia
First Edition
1 3 5 7 9 10 8 6 4 2
H106-93335-14015

Library of Congress Cataloging-in-Publication Data

Sitomer, Alan Lawrence.
  Daddy and the zigzagging bedtime story / written by Alan Lawrence
Sitomer ; illustrated by Abby Carter.—First edition.
      pages cm
  Summary: When Jake and Jenny say they are bored with all their books and retold tales, their father makes up a new bedtime story about a princess who drives a monster truck and battles aliens aided by a cupcake-baking unicorn.
  ISBN 978-1-4231-8420-1 (hardback)
  [1. Storytelling—Fiction. 2. Bedtime—Fiction. 3. Father and
child—Fiction. 4. Humorous stories.] I. Carter, Abby, illustrator. II. Title.
  PZ7.S6228Dag 2014
  [E]—dc23   2013040738

Designed by Tanya Ross-Hughes
Text is set in 16-point Chaloops
Reinforced binding

Visit www.disneyhyperionbooks.com

Dedicated to my two little Pickle Quackers

"All right, you little Pickle Quackers,
it's bedtime."

"Can I pick the book tonight?"

"No, I want to!"

"But it's my turn."

"No, it's mine."

"Just hold on a moment.
Daddy has a simple solution.
I'll choose the book tonight."

"Once upon a time . . ."

"Bor-ring,"
Jake said.

"Heard it," Jenny added.
"Like two million times."

"All right, how about **this one?**

"A long time ago, far, far away . . ."

"Older than a dinosaur egg," Jenny said.

"How about **this?**"

"Nope."

"What about **this one?**"

"Or **this** one?

"You know, when **I** was a kid . . ."

"Daddy, did they have electricity
when you were our age?"

"Maybe another night."

"I wish Mommy had no friends
so she could be home tonight
instead of out to dinner."

"How about if Daddy **invents** a story instead?"

"But the truck was covered with shiny purple and silver sparkles made from magic fairy dust.

"Of course, the magic fairy dust allowed the monster truck

to fly, so it could . . .

"... battle the evil Space Aliens of Doom!"

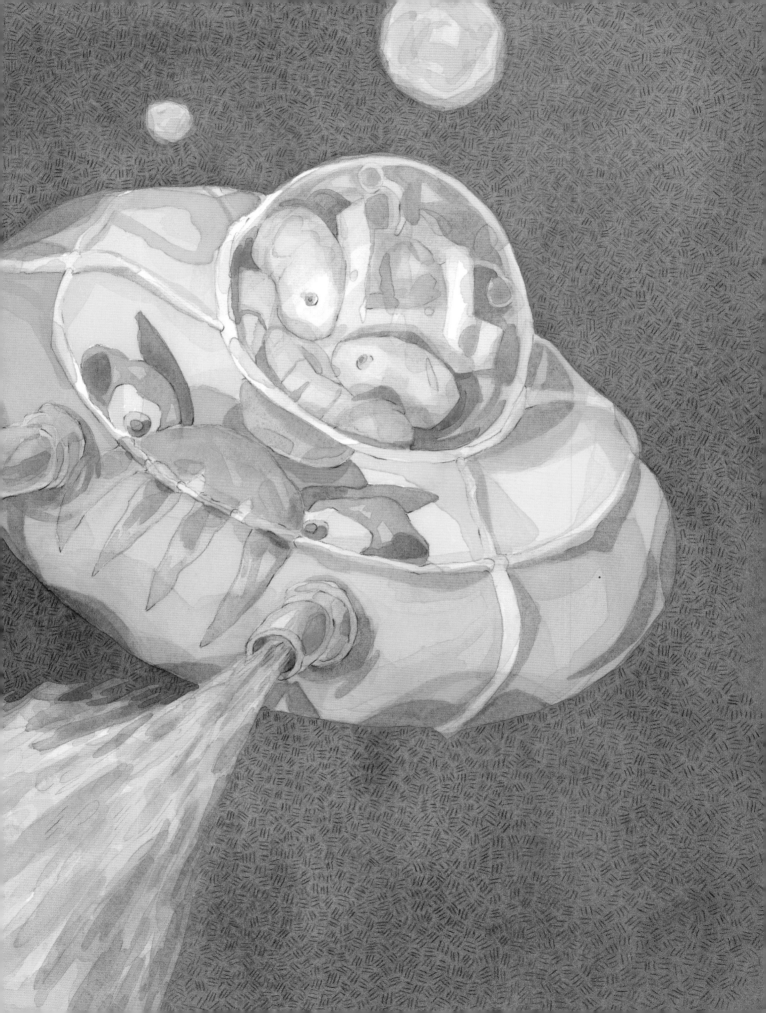

"All with the help of an enchanted unicorn who baked vanilla cupcakes.

"But the leader of the aliens, Zorgon the Fire-Burper, would **never** stop until he

"So the brave princess pulled out her laser saber,

slapped on her X-ray invisibility glasses, canceled her playdate with Emma, and hailed her army of adorable orphan   kitty cats!"

"But the fearsome Zorgon would not be stopped . . .

. . . so he summoned the famous Kung-Fu Cabal of Sneezing Pigs and began to launch missiles filled with corn and the eyeballs of dead spiders. Yet the heroic princess—who had grown up without parents, uncles, or even an iPad—retaliated with a surprise black-belt ballet-slipper spinning-thermonuclear side rumple-dumple kick (that she'd learned from her mentor, Cuddles the Ninja Puppy) and . . .

BOOM!

The princess defeated Zorgon!"

"And everyone lived happily ever after."

"Daddy, can you tell us
one more story?"

"Tomorrow, my little Pickle Quackers.

"Nighty-night . . . and don't let Zorgon the Fire-Burper bite."